The Short and Incredibly Happy Life of Riley

Colin Thompson & Amy Lissiat

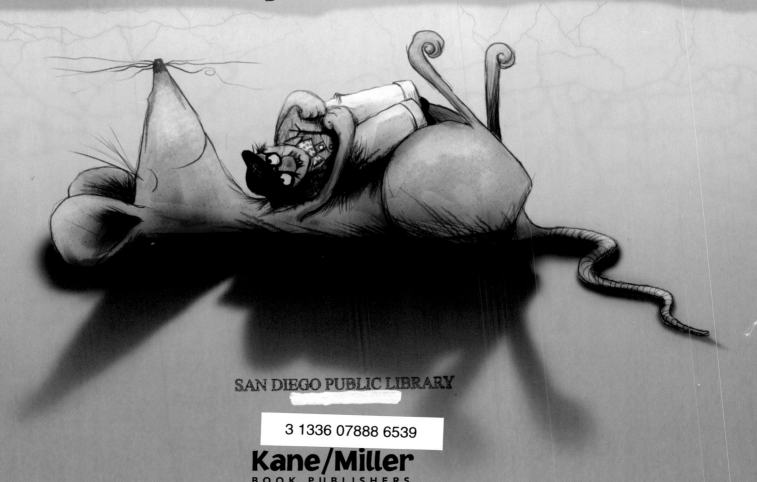

Kane/Miller
BOOK PUBLISHERS

Everyone wants to live forever.

They want to be happy and healthy.

Some of these things are actually quite difficult, but some of them are really easy, which might seem surprising because most people hardly manage any of them. At least not all of the time.

None of this bothered Riley.

Riley had been born happy. His earliest memory was being with his brothers and sisters and mom in a big bed with plenty of food and no rain.

He was always happy, even when he was asleep.

He was beautiful and everyone loved him. He was the best and so were his brothers and sisters and mom.

All Riley wanted was some fruit and maybe a couple of slugs on Tuesday or Friday or now and then.

People, of course, want more than that, which is a shame because it's about all you need, apart from a cup of tea and some toast and maybe not the slug.

People want double-fudge-chocolate-caviar-sausage-
gourmet-jumbo-size-baby-cow-sheep-chicken-with-extra-
thick-whipped-cream-and-msg-sauce-burgers.

Some of which is gross, some cruel and most, unhealthy.

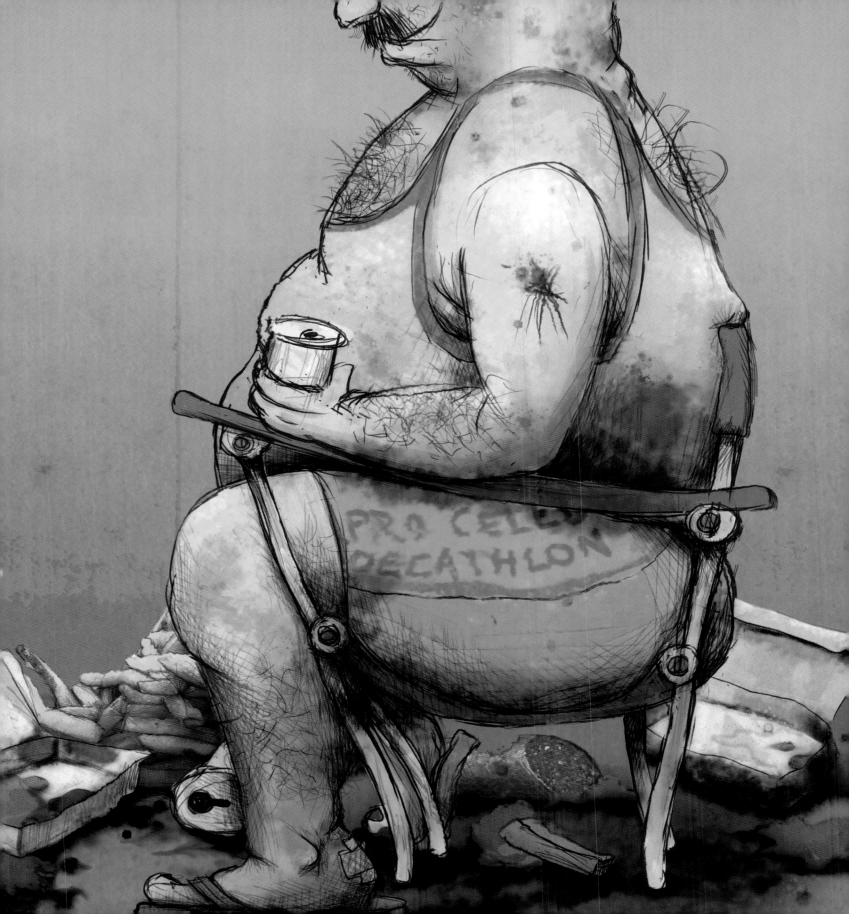

They want microwave-video-dvd-sms-internet-big-car-cost-more-than-yours-gold-diamond-electronic-gigabyte-fastest-biggest-and-smallest-machines.

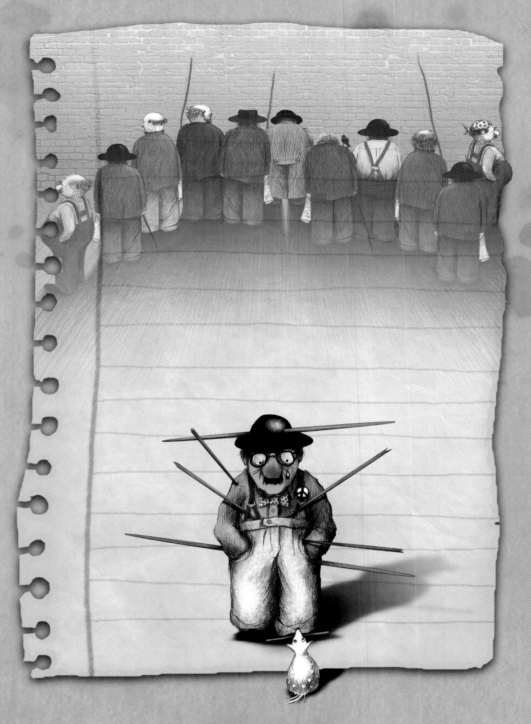

Ｐeople, of course, should never be allowed to have sticks with pointy ends, because they stick them into each other.

They want to be taller-shorter-thinner-here-but-much-bigger-there-curly-straight-younger-older-less-spotty-moustache-smooth-skin-golden-sun-tan-gorgeous-irresistible-not-bald-and-famous-in-a-painting.

The only place Riley ever wanted to be was here, which he always was.

People, of course, want to be everywhere.

They want to go to the seaside-ski-resort-paradise-dream-world-castaway-exclusive-you-must-be-really-rich-if-you-can-afford-to-come-here-plaza-luxury-get-away-from-it-all-anywhere-but-here-theme-park.

Riley fell in love with the first girl he met. He thought she was perfect and the most beautiful girl he had ever seen. They had lots and lots of perfect children and all lived happily ever after, except Kevin who got hit by a bus but was still happy because he never saw it coming.

People fall in love all over the place.

They fall in love with themselves and as many other people as they can. They want to spend the rest of their lives for at least a month with the most-beautiful-funniest-curviest-clever-but-not-as-clever-as-me-exciting-I-wonder-what-I-ever-saw-in-him/her-my-wife/husband/partner/dog-doesn't-understand-me-do-you-come-here-often-anyone-everyone-in-the-world.

And one of the silly things about life is that people, who spend so much time not eating what they really want, in places where they don't want to be, with people they don't like, usually live for quite a long time. Whereas Riley, who spends all the time eating his favorite food in his favorite place with his favorite friends, only lives for a very short time.

This is why it's never a good idea for people to compare their lives to animals.

You will only end up feeling depressed ...

because realizing that rats have a better life
than you do, is really, really sad.

And the answer is very simple really – you just have to be happy with a lot less.

Release your inner Riley

Kane/Miller Book Publishers, Inc.
First American Edition 2007
by Kane/Miller Book Publishers, Inc.
La Jolla, California

First published in Australia in 2005 by Lothian Books (now Hachette Livre Australia Pty Ltd.)
This edition is published by arrangement with Hachette Livre Australia Pty Ltd.

Kane/Miller Book Publishers, Inc.
P.O. Box 8515
La Jolla, CA 92038
www.kanemiller.com

Library of Congress Control Number: 2007921053
Printed and bound in China
1 2 3 4 5 6 7 8 9 10

ISBN: 978-1-933605-50-0

Designed by Colin Thompson
Illustration technique: Photoshop on an Apple Macintosh